SUPER DC HEROES

BATMAN™

THE FOG OF FEAR

WRITTEN BY
MARTIN POWELL

ILLUSTRATED BY
ERIK DOESCHER,
MIKE DECARLO, AND
LEE LOUGHRIDGE

BATMAN CREATED BY
BOB KANE

STONE ARCH BOOKS
MINNEAPOLIS SAN DIEGO

Published by Stone Arch Books in 2013
A Capstone Imprint
1710 Roe Crest Drive
North Mankato, MN 56003
www.capstonepub.com

STAR29440

Cataloging-in-Publication Data is available at the Library of Congress website.

ISBN: 978-1-4342-5817-5 (paperback)

Summary: A two-story flipbook featuring BATMAN and SUPERMAN, DC Comics' greatest heroes.

Printed in China
092012 006926

TABLE OF CONTENTS

CHAPTER 1

THE FOG OF FEAR

Darkness crawled across the morning sky like a giant bat from a nightmare. The residents of Gotham City stared up from the streets, or peeked out of windows, for a sign of the vanished sun. Somehow, mysteriously, it had become twilight before noon. A sudden fear of the dark gripped the entire city.

Then, a bright light sliced through the shadows. The Bat-Signal shined against the darkened clouds. It was a welcome sight for their frightened eyes.

"Never dreamed I'd have to shine the Bat-Signal in the daytime," Commissioner Gordon said. He stood on the police department rooftop. "I hope Batman sees it . . . wherever he is."

The towering smokestacks of the Gotham City power plant spit a thick cloud of black fog high above the skyline. Creating its own eclipse, the darkness draped over the panicked streets. It grew like a great uncoiling snake. Before long, the bright morning spring air was as dark as midnight.

The citizens of Gotham would have been even more afraid, if they'd seen the figure atop the highest smokestack. Dressed in tatters and thin as a skeleton, the weird being shed small scraps of straw with every footstep.

He pulled a glowing jack-o'-lantern from a bag in his hand. He had already tossed several others down into the smoldering smokestack. The ragged man cackled a laugh like the sound of breaking glass.

"Trick or treat, Gotham City," the Scarecrow cried, ready to drop a pumpkin into the next chimney. "Today is Halloween — six months early!"

Schinggg!

Suddenly, a Batarang flew through the air and knocked the pumpkin out of the Scarecrow's grasp. A black-cloaked creature appeared out of nowhere, his eyes burning white-hot through the slits of his cowl.

"Not in my city," the Batman said.

Now it was the Scarecrow's turn to be afraid.

"Too late, Batman!" the Scarecrow shrieked. "You've lost already!"

Flinging his sleeves, the Scarecrow threw a clump of stinging straw into Batman's face. Like a bundle of living rags, the villain dashed around the narrow rim of the smokestack. Escape was the only thing on his evil mind.

Gripping a hooked rope, the Scarecrow prepared for his descent. Twice, he rapidly glanced behind. His eyes grew wide with surprise through the holes of his mask. Where was Batman? Among the drifting ribbons of the thick fog the Scarecrow's enemy was nowhere to be seen.

The Scarecrow quickly hurried down the long rope. An evil smile crossed his lips. Had Batman fallen to his doom? Perhaps he was finally rid of his enemy forever.

THWACK!

Fast as lightning, a Batarang struck the Scarecrow's glove. His fingers released the rope. The villain waved his arms helplessly and fell toward the earth below.

Batman appeared through the curtain of darkness, swinging on his Batrope. His cape flapped in the wind. In a single motion, the Caped Crusader snatched the Scarecrow from his fall.

"Don't be afraid, Scarecrow," Batman said. He gripped a small device on the rope that lowered them both gently to the ground. "I'll make sure you're safe," he said, "inside a strong jail cell."

CHAPTER 2

SINISTER SECRETS

Commissioner Gordon paced anxiously. His shoes scraped the tarred rooftop of Police Headquarters. The creeping darkness of the Scarecrow's black fog still covered the streets in shadows. Gordon was beginning to fear for his city.

"You're sure this stuff isn't poisonous, Batman?" the Commissioner asked.

The Dark Knight was standing near him on the edge of the rooftop. His fluttering cape blended with the black fog.

"My lab tests confirm that this fog is not poisonous," Batman replied. "Because it's heavier than air, it will linger in Gotham City until the wind carries it out to sea. The weather will change in our favor in a few days. Until then, everyone has to get used to living in the shadows."

Commissioner Gordon frowned at the dark fog.

"That's easy for you to say, Batman," he said. "Still, I feel sorry for anyone scared of the dark."

Batman's eyes narrowed. "That's just it," he said. "The Scarecrow works through fear. Even after I captured him at the power plant, he seemed strangely sure of himself. It's as if he still has some fearful secret that I haven't solved yet."

"Gotham City is safe because of you," said Commissioner Gordon. "At least the threat of the Scarecrow is over, and he is safely locked up."

The Dark Knight shook his head thoughtfully. "It's not over yet, old friend," he said quietly.

"That's just what I'm afraid of," said the commissioner.

• • •

It was always dark in the Batcave, secretly located beneath Wayne Manor. Later that afternoon, inside the hidden cavern, Batman removed his cape and cowl, revealing the face of billionaire Bruce Wayne. Wayne peered into a high-powered microscope. He fought a yawn, rubbed his tired eyes, and got back to work.

Behind Bruce rose a tall, dark set of stairs. Alfred the butler was coming down the stairs into the underground laboratory. "Miss Kyle called, Master Bruce. She's waiting to meet you for lunch at the restaurant," said Alfred.

Bruce prepared a thin orange-colored slice upon a glass slide. He added a drop of a glowing chemical.

"Call her back with my apologies, Alfred," he said. "It's going to be dark as night in Gotham City for the next few days. Commissioner Gordon's policemen are working 24-hour shifts. Batman can do no less."

Alfred peeked over Bruce's shoulder. He stared at a strange orange vegetable sitting on the table.

"Isn't it a bit early for carving pumpkins, sir?" Alfred asked.

Bruce smiled. "This belonged to the Scarecrow," he explained. "He filled these pumpkins with a secret chemical before tossing them into the power plant smokestacks. The result was the black fog that is still plaguing the city."

"Well, sir," offered Alfred, "I'll admit this fog is troubling. However, it's hardly the same kind of trick the Scarecrow has used against you in the past."

Bruce rose quickly, grabbing his black cowl and cloak. "Exactly," he said. Bruce filled the compartments of his Utility Belt. "There's more to this black fog than meets the eye. And, one way or the other, the Scarecrow is going to tell me its secret."

Arkham Asylum was like a madhouse from another world. Locked within its electrified iron gates lived the deadliest criminals ever known. Even in the daylight, the building looked like a bad dream. The black fog added even more to its eeriness.

The headlights of the Batmobile sliced through the inky clouds of fog. The front guards saluted as Batman stepped out of the vehicle. He passed into the dreadful place without a word. Caged doors opened before him with a motorized hum. The Dark Knight knew his way through the twisted corridors all too well.

"If I'd known you were coming, I'd have baked a Bat-cake!" a voice giggled from behind a cell door.

Batman stopped and glared at the white face pressed against the bars.

"Joker," he said through gritted teeth.

The Joker's blood-red lips continued to curl upward toward his yellow eyes. Batman's face remained like stone, unsmiling. Upon reflex, his gloved fists tightly clenched.

"Hey, Bats! When are you gonna bring back the sunshine?" the Joker said. A chuckle hissed between his teeth.

"What's the matter, Joker?" asked Batman. "Afraid of the dark?"

"You gotta be kidding, Bat-brain!" the killer clown gleefully cried. "I just want to know when you're gonna ruin the Scarecrow's party! He's been raving about his 'Crime of the Century' for hours. Such a bore. Frankly, just between us boys, I think he's nutty as a filbert!"

Batman whirled from the cell. He had to focus on the problem at hand. The mystery of the Scarecrow was waiting to be solved.

Jonathan Crane had once been a brilliant professor of psychology. He specialized in the study of fear. That was before his mind snapped and he turned to crime. As the Scarecrow, Crane had always been defeated by Batman, no matter how ingenious his crimes. This time Crane was certain things were going to be different.

Crane looked almost harmless without his fearsome costume. Tall and thin with an evil smirk on his face, he sat in his cell quietly reading. Batman studied him silently for several minutes.

"I'm only going to ask you this once, Crane," the Dark Knight warned. "What's the secret of the black fog?"

Crane continued reading, as if he'd heard nothing. Then he smugly smiled.

"You'll know soon enough, Batman," the evil genius replied. "Now, if you'll excuse me, I'm trying to broaden my mind."

Batman's brain worked at top speed. He read the titles of the volumes on Crane's crammed bookshelves. Many of the books were old. Some were ancient. Most of them seemed to be about the so-called "four elements": fire, water, earth, and air. Hundreds of years ago, men called alchemists believed that the world was made of just these four ingredients.

Could Crane's formula be related to the four elements? wondered Batman.

Immediately, the Dark Knight had the answer.

SCARECROW
CRANE

'Earth' would equal the jack-o'-lanterns. 'Fire' was added from the power plant smokestacks. 'Air' joined the mix, forming the black fog. One element was missing: A single ingredient that would turn the black fog deadly.

"Water!" Batman exclaimed.

RUMMMMMMMMMBLE! Batman's blood ran cold. His sharp ears caught the rumble of an approaching thunderstorm.

From out of Crane's thin lips came the Scarecrow's awful laugh.

CHAPTER 3

CLOUDED BY FEAR

Commission Gordon leaned against his office desk to steady himself. The news Batman had brought was shocking. Gordon knew that the Dark Knight was almost never wrong.

"If what you're saying is true, Batman," he said, "then all of Gotham is about to be scared to death!"

"There's no doubt about it," Batman assured him. "When I visited Scarecrow's cell, I solved the mystery of his plan. I detected the poison in his formula."

"Once this black fog is mixed with water," Batman continued, "all who breathe it will experience their most dreadful fears. Unless we act quickly, the city is doomed to be trapped forever inside their worst nightmares."

Gordon went to the window and glanced outside. It was just past three o'clock in the afternoon, yet the sky was still dark as midnight. The Bat-Signal was still burning against the black clouds, just as the Commissioner had ordered. Its presence gave looters and other criminals second thoughts. The Bat-Signal also gave hope to Gotham City's honest citizens.

The approaching thunderstorm growled in the distance. Jagged shards of lightning flashed on the horizon.

"This coming storm will drench the city in terror," Gordon said. He thumped his fist hard against the sill. "Is there anything that can be done?"

Batman nodded. "We can clean the air of the black fog before the rain begins," he said. He sounded confident, in spite of the odds against him.

Commissioner Gordon spun on his heels. He greatly respected his friend, but this idea sounded impossible.

"But how, Batman?" he asked. "You said that there won't be enough wind in Gotham for days. How can we possibly speed up Mother Nature?"

The Caped Crusader moved to the window and opened it. He fired a grapple and rope to a neighboring building.

"With our courage and our wits," Batman remarked.

FWOOOSHHHHHH!! He swung away, disappearing into the murky air.

Batman swooped high above the streets of Gotham City. People down below saw the shadow of a huge bat flying through the strange fog. None of them knew it was really the Caped Crusader.

Batman used his rope and grappling device to swing from building to building. His goal was a tall, white skyscraper near the edge of the city. Inside the building was a high-tech laboratory owned by one of the world's greatest scientists, Dr. Kirk Langstrom. Batman hoped that Langstrom's science would be strong enough to defeat the Scarecrow's evil formula.

As the Dark Knight swooped through the fog, tiny water droplets collected on his armored suit. The mist pressed cold and damp against his cowl.

Without warning, Batman's rope changed shape. Instead of a thin silken cord, he was holding onto a deadly boa constrictor.

HISSSSSSS

"What —?" yelled Batman. He released his grip on the snake and began to fall.

Batman shot a grappling hook toward another nearby building. ZING! Just in time, the new rope pulled him upward. He barely missed hitting a statue coming out from the side of an office building.

That was close, thought Batman. *But what is going on?*

Again, his rope transformed. This time it turned into a super sticky web. A monstrous spider snapped its drooling jaws. Its giant head thrust toward the startled hero.

"You can't be real," said Batman, shaking his head. He shot out his feet and swung quickly around his rope, building up speed. Then he aimed his boots at the fearsome mouth of the spider. Instead of feeling the impact, Batman's feet met nothing but air.

It's an illusion, he thought. *It must be the mist. There's just enough water in the air to combine with the black smoke and make me see things.*

Batman frowned. *If this is how the Scarecrow's fog can affect the brain with just a little water, then the rainstorm will create a total panic.*

Batman increased his speed and swung toward the white skyscraper. Things were worse than he imagined.

CHAPTER 4

THE LIVING NIGHTMARE

"I knew I could count on you, Kirk," Batman said. He shook the scientist's hand.

Kirk Langstrom stood in his white lab coat, a deep contrast to Batman's black and grey Batsuit. Still, the two men shared at least two traits. Both were brilliant. Both wanted to save their city.

"You cured me, Batman. I owe you everything," Langstrom replied. "When I experimented with the bat-serum, I turned into the monster, Man-Bat."

"You were the only one who helped me," said Langstrom. "I'll never forget that."

The Dark Knight remembered those frightening nights when his friend had changed into a powerful creature. Although not truly evil, the Man-Bat was wild and uncontrollable. Those memories were like a nightmare to both men.

"This is Gotham's only hope," Batman stated. "You are the world's greatest living expert on bats."

"Takes one to know one, I guess," Langstrom said. He smiled, almost sadly, as he unveiled his experimental machine.

The device on Langstrom's laboratory workbench looked like something from a science-fiction movie. It was made of blinking lights and coiling wires.

Batman noticed that Langstrom himself stared at the machine with dread. As much as the scientist wanted to help, he was still hiding something.

"I haven't tested it yet," Langstrom said quietly. "But if it works, the machine should send out a high-pitch sound. The sound can only be heard by the sensitive ears of bats. Bats are the most common mammal in North America. Millions of them will be awakened by this sound, flying to wherever it leads them."

Batman was impressed. The machine was exactly what he needed.

"That's all I need to know," he said, reaching for the device.

The Dark Knight slowly flipped a small switch.

The machine glowed, then started to hum. Although Batman could feel only a slight vibration in the air, Langstrom's ears immediately began to ache.

FLAP! FLAP! FLAP! FLAP!

Within minutes, hundreds of bats swooped and fluttered against the window of the lab.

"It works!" cried Langstrom.

Batman turned off the machine, well satisfied.

"It's perfect, Kirk," he said. "I have just enough time to get this machine back to the Batcave before the thunderstorm starts."

There was an eerie silence in the room. Langstrom had retreated into a far corner, away from the harsh light in the lab.

Batman was alarmed by the sounds of the scientist's heavy breaths. He took a step toward his friend.

"Kirk? Are you all right?" he asked.

No answer came from the dark corner. Then Batman heard the sounds of more rapid breathing. He heard a slow ripping of cloth. Then he saw a sudden spreading of monstrous wings.

The Man-Bat had returned. Langstrom had been transformed by the effect of his sound machine!

The Dark Knight braced himself as he saw the burning red eyes glare at him. The creature sprang forward. Batman was driven back by the muscular weight of the monster. He crashed backwards through tables of shattering glass.

There was no more expert fighter in the world than the Batman. But for a moment, even his fists were useless against the strength and speed of the Man-Bat.

The beast's claws gripped Batman's throat with a blur of motion. Sharp teeth gleamed behind the gruesome growl. Batman's brain was spinning, close to blacking out. His gloved fingers groped for his Utility Belt, his only chance.

FLASH! A bright flare shined in Batman's hand. The Man-Bat howled in rage. It flung itself through the window.

The Dark Knight caught his breath. He watched the Man-Bat escape into the gloomy sky, carried by its giant wings.

"You feared this would happen, didn't you?" Batman said to himself. "Kirk, why didn't you tell me?"

CHAPTER 5

BATMAN VS MAN-BAT

Less than an hour later, the Batplane screamed out of the Gotham sky. The storm was almost upon the city. There wasn't a moment to lose.

Kirk Langstrom's amazing invention was wired into an amplifier within the plane's cockpit. All Batman needed to do was press the switch . . . and hope.

The sound was much too high for the Dark Knight's human ears. Several minutes passed before he knew for sure that it was operating. Then, suddenly, there they were.

"Bats!"

The bats obeyed the sound machine, following close behind the Batplane. They came in an endless stream, thousands and thousands of them. Countless tiny wings flapped through the air. Soon, the black fog softened to a grey. The sky was alive with the swarm of fluttering wings.

The Batplane streaked through the clouds. It rocketed above rooftops and sliced between buildings. The bats followed, sweeping away the fog with every beat of their leathery wings. In a few minutes the Scarecrow's black fog was no more.

Batman turned off the sound machine. The swarm of bats cleared the skies and returned to their hidden lairs. The Dark Knight was about to breathe a sigh of relief when another threat struck from the sky.

WHAM! Something hard collided against the hull of the Batplane. Batman saw the jagged wings and glowing eyes of his attacker.

The Man-Bat had also answered the call of the machine. In a mindless rage, the Man-Bat struck the Batplane. Batman fought hard to regain control. He had to take this battle down to the ground, out of the Man-Bat's element. His sharp eyes found a safe place to land — an old cemetery outside of the city.

The Batplane glided down among the twisted trees and tombstones. It came to a stop just as the rain started to fall.

Leaping from the cockpit, Batman peered skyward. The rain poured down, making it hard to see.

The Man-Bat was fast and strong. The Dark Knight knew he would only get one chance to defeat the beast.

CRAAAAACK!!

A furious flash of lightning revealed the Man-Bat, swooping out of the sky like a prehistoric monster. Batman dropped and rolled away as the creature's deadly talons grabbed only mud. Again the flying fiend shot toward Batman like a demon, but its claws found only open air. A spinning kick to the creature's chest finally brought the Man-Bat to earth.

The monster rose up from the mud, towering above Batman. Pain and hatred grew in Man-Bat's mind. It let out a terrible snarl. Batman's right hand went to his Utility Belt, retrieving an item, which he hid behind his glove.

"Kirk!" Batman said. He tried to calm the beast. "I want to help you. Kirk, don't you know me?"

The Man-Bat's wild eyes softened a moment. The creature tilted its head in confusion. Batman approached the creature slowly. Deadly as Man-Bat might be, Batman had to get close enough to touch.

A sudden clap of thunder startled the beast. ROOAAARRR!!

Its clawed wings wrapped tightly around Batman's throat. Nothing could break the monstrous grip. It was too strong. But the Dark Knight's right hand was free, and that was all he needed. He made a quick move, pressing a sharp object against the creature's hide.

The Man-Bat released its stranglehold in a snap. It appeared to grow dizzy and staggered. Finally, it dropped to its shaggy knees.

The Batman returned the object to his Utility Belt. It was a needle that had contained the antidote to the Man-Bat formula.

Before Batman's eyes, the giant beast seemed to shrink. Its fur slowly melted away. The huge wings grew smaller and disappeared. In a few moments, scientist Kirk Langstrom crouched in the creature's place. Batman carefully helped his friend stand.

"Batman?" Langstrom asked. "What have I done?" He remembered nothing from the past few hours.

Batman placed a grateful hand on Langstrom's shoulder. "You saved the city, Kirk," he said softly. "The black fog is gone, blown away by the wings of bats. Your machine worked just as you said. You're a hero."

The storm was over. The rain had ended, and the Scarecrow's evil nightmares vanished with the coming sunshine.

"I had a terrible dream about Man-Bat," said Langstrom, confused. "I was afraid he had come back. Afraid he'd try to hurt you."

Batman smiled. "Nothing to be afraid of now," he said.

It was going to be a beautiful day in Gotham City.

SUPERMAN

METEOR OF DOOM

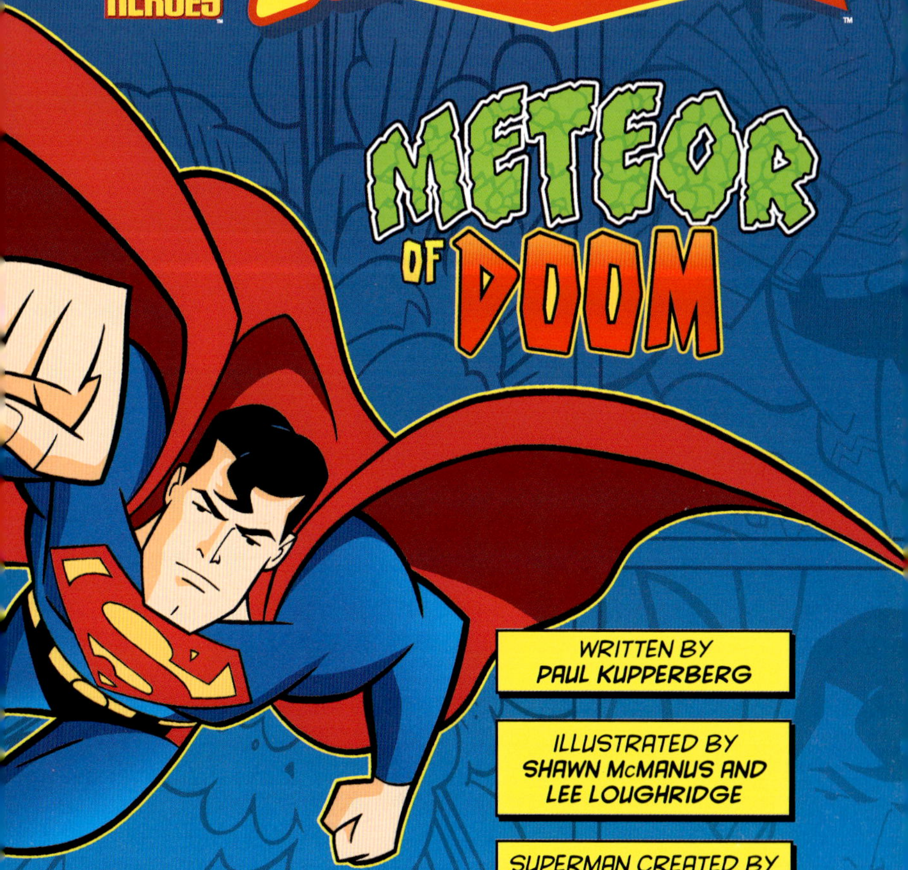

WRITTEN BY
PAUL KUPPERBERG

ILLUSTRATED BY
SHAWN McMANUS AND
LEE LOUGHRIDGE

SUPERMAN CREATED BY
JERRY SIEGEL AND
JOE SHUSTER

STONE ARCH BOOKS
MINNEAPOLIS SAN DIEGO

Published by Stone Arch Books in 2013
A Capstone Imprint
1710 Roe Crest Drive
North Mankato, MN 56003
www.capstonepub.com

STAR29440

Cataloging-in-Publication Data is available at the Library of Congress website.

ISBN: 978-1-4342-5817-5 (paperback)

Summary: A two-story flipbook featuring BATMAN and SUPERMAN, DC Comics' greatest heroes.

Printed in China
092012 006926

TABLE OF CONTENTS

CHAPTER 1

SURPRISE FROM THE SKY

LexCorp Tower stood in the center of Metropolis. It was one of the tallest buildings in the city and was named for its owner, Lex Luthor. Luthor was one of the richest businessmen in the world. Thousands of people in Metropolis worked for his companies.

Luthor enjoyed impressing people with his money. When he wanted to announce news about his company to reporters, he did it from his private garden on the roof of LexCorp Tower.

As the sun shined in the sky, Luthor stood in front of a microphone in the garden. Nearby was a large box-shaped device. It was covered with a dark blue sheet.

Clark Kent and Lois Lane were reporters for the Metropolis *Daily Planet* newspaper. They were just two of the many reporters there to hear Luthor's announcement. Clark had a pad of paper and pen in his hand to take notes.

"I wonder what Luthor is planning?" Lois said. "You know how he likes to make a big deal out of everything he does."

"He is a show-off," Clark admitted. "I just hope he doesn't take too long. I'm supposed to be at S.T.A.R. Laboratories. I'm covering the return of the Deep Space Probe for tomorrow's paper."

"The space mission?" Lois asked. "Aren't they bringing back meteors from orbit around Mars?"

"Yes," Clark said. "These will be the first meteors ever brought back from space! Before now, the only meteors scientists have been able to study were the ones that fell to Earth."

"Ladies and gentlemen," Luthor spoke into the microphone. "Thank you all for coming. As you know, LexCorp is always looking for ways to help the people of Metropolis. I am pleased to introduce our latest invention . . . the LexCorp Solar Generator!"

Luthor grasped the edge of the sheet that covered the mysterious box-shaped device. He paused for a moment and then tugged on the sheet.

The sheet slid off the device, revealing a golden box with a shiny top. The top sparkled in the afternoon sunlight. Reporters leaned in for a closer look at the device. Photographers took pictures.

"The Solar Generator is a battery that stores energy from the sun," Luthor told the curious reporters. "That energy can be used to supply electricity for your entire house. And it costs only pennies a day!"

The excited reporters began to shout questions at Luthor. Clark Kent was not one of them. Instead, he stood still. His eyes were raised to the sky.

"What's wrong, Clark?" Lois asked.

"I thought I heard something," Clark said.

"I don't hear anything," said Lois.

Lois did not know that Clark Kent had secret abilities. He could hear and do things ordinary people could not.

Clark pointed upward. "There!" he said.

Lois thought he was pointing at a flock of birds flying toward the roof. As they came closer, she saw they were not birds. They were men — three of them — each wearing a rocket-powered flying suit!

Before Lois could say anything, Clark pushed her toward the elevators.

"Quick, Lois," he said. "You should get inside and call the police!"

"*You* call the police," Lois said. "I'm not going to miss out on this story!"

With his super-vision, Clark could see that the flying men were carrying energy blasters. There was no time to waste.

Clark ran to the elevator. As soon as the doors closed, the mild-mannered reporter pulled open his shirt. Beneath it was a blue uniform. It was marked with the famous red and yellow "S" symbol.

"This looks like a job," Clark said to himself, "for Superman!"

As Clark Kent changed into his Superman uniform, the flying men swooped down from the sky. They began firing their energy blasters at the people gathered on the rooftop.

BOOM! The first shot caused a bed of rare flowers to explode in a shower of dirt and flower petals.

BOOM! The next one shattered Luthor's Solar Generator into a thousand pieces of metal and glass.

KA-BOOM! KA-BOOM!

Two more blasts melted the microphone where Luthor had been standing just a moment before.

Luthor shook his fist at the flying men. "How dare you!" he yelled over the sound of the blasts. "Don't you know who I am?"

The reporters were also yelling, but they were shouting in fear and panic. While the other reporters were running away, Lois Lane ran toward the attack. She pulled a digital camera from her purse.

This is turning out to be a better story than I imagined! Lois thought.

Lois aimed the camera at one of the attackers. **FLASH!** She took a picture of the flying man. Then he turned and pointed at her.

"There she is!" the flying man yelled to his companions. "Get her!"

"Uh-oh!" Lois said. She started to run. The flying men were speeding toward her from all sides. She was trapped!

CHAPTER 2

ATTACK ON METROPOLIS

The flying men were speeding toward Lois. There was nowhere to run. Then Superman swooped down from the sky and landed in front of her.

"Looks like you could use a hand, Lois," a familiar voice said.

Lois gasped in relief. "Superman!" she said.

The armored men were surprised by the sudden appearance of the super hero, but they did not slow down.

CRUNCH! The closest attacker smashed into Superman's chest. The man's armor broke open like a tin can. Superman did not budge from the impact.

Superman was born on the distant planet Krypton. He had been sent to Earth by his parents when Krypton exploded. The Earth's yellow sun made his alien body super-strong and super-fast. It also gave him other superpowers. He was invulnerable, which meant he could not be hurt like normal people. Only magic and kryptonite, a rare, glowing green rock from his home planet, could harm the Man of Steel.

Superman looked up at the second flying man. He narrowed his eyes. In an instant, beams of heat-vision flashed from the hero's eyes. BZZZT!

The beams struck the small rocket engine on the back of the flyer's armored suit. The engine caught fire. POP! POP! It sputtered and shut off. The armored man yelled in surprise. He fell to the rooftop like a rock.

"Superman, look out!" cried Lois.

The Man of Steel turned. He saw the last flying man aiming his energy blaster at him. Superman smiled and took a deep breath. He blew out a mighty blast from his super-powered lungs.

THWOOOOOMMM!! The flying man was caught like a leaf in a hurricane. With a frightened scream, he was sent tumbling backward through the air. He landed with a crash, many miles away, right in front of the Metropolis police headquarters.

Superman turned to Lois and asked, “Are you all right, Miss Lane?”

“I am now, thanks to you,” Lois said.

Lex Luthor came storming over to Superman and shouted, “There’s nothing to thank him for, Ms. Lane! If he had gotten here faster, those villains wouldn’t have destroyed my Solar Generator! And my beautiful garden is ruined!”

“You’re just angry because Superman had to rescue you, Luthor,” Lois said. “It’s no secret how jealous you are that everyone in Metropolis thinks Superman’s a bigger hero than you!”

“Lex Luthor is jealous of no man!” said the angry businessman.

“No, but you’re sure jealous of a *super* man!” Lois said with a sly smile.

Superman was staring at the wreckage of the Solar Generator.

"Hmm," Superman said, before turning to Luthor. "I'm sorry I couldn't save your new machine, Luthor. Fortunately, no one was hurt in the attack."

"What about my garden?" Luthor bellowed.

"You can always grow new flowers," said the Man of Steel. "Now, if you'll excuse me, I have another appointment." He did not say that it was with S.T.A.R. Laboratories to report on the return of the Deep Space Probe as Clark Kent.

"Thanks again, Superman," Lois called as he flew away.

Superman waved and said, "Always happy to help, Lois."

As he flew away, Superman knew that it wasn't jealousy that caused Luthor to hate him. It was because of the dark secret that Luthor kept hidden from the people of Metropolis. Behind his reputation as a businessman and inventor, Lex Luthor was the mastermind of a worldwide criminal empire!

So far, Luthor had been too smart to leave any evidence. Superman couldn't prove he was a criminal. Still, Luthor knew that if anyone could ever prove he was guilty, it would be the Man of Steel. Because of that, Luthor had vowed to destroy Superman.

Superman's thoughts were cut short by a sudden sound.

BEEP! BEEP! BEEP!

It was a special sound that only Superman's ears could hear. It was made by a signaling device that he had given to a close friend. Hearing it now meant only one thing.

Jimmy Olsen was in trouble!

CHAPTER 3

METAL MONSTER

WHAM! A giant metal foot bigger than a car smashed into the sidewalk right next to Jimmy Olsen. With a loud yelp of surprise, Jimmy jumped out of its way. The giant foot had missed him by inches!

The young man flattened himself against the side of a building. He looked up, and up, and up. His eyes traveled from the car-sized foot to a metal leg that was at least 30 feet tall. Then he saw a robot with gleaming eyes and arms as long as fire hoses.

"Wow!" Jimmy whispered in shocked surprise.

Only moments earlier, the young *Daily Planet* photographer had been strolling down the street. He was on his way to meet Clark Kent at the S.T.A.R. Laboratories Building. S.T.A.R. stood for Scientific and Technological Advanced Research. The smartest scientists from all over the world worked for S.T.A.R. They created scientific and medical marvels for the benefit of people everywhere.

Jimmy had been excited about this assignment. He was going to be allowed to take the very first pictures of the meteors being brought back from Mars on the Deep Space Probe!

But for now, the meteors would have to wait.

As soon as the giant robot had appeared in the street, Jimmy touched a signal button on his special wristwatch. Superman had given it to him. The button activated a supersonic danger signal that only Superman could hear.

CLICK! CLICK! Jimmy started snapping pictures of the robot. For a moment, the metal monster didn't notice. Seventy feet up in the air, its massive head turned back and forth. It seemed to be searching for something. Jimmy kept shooting pictures. CLICK! CLICK!

Suddenly, through the camera's viewfinder, Jimmy saw the robot's giant green eyes staring down at him. By the time he had lowered the camera from his face, the robot's metal hand was already reaching for him!

Jimmy gulped in fear and turned to run. He knew he could not possibly run fast enough to escape that giant hand. He had only one hope.

"Superman!" Jimmy exclaimed.

The Man of Steel arrived in the nick of time. He snatched Jimmy Olsen away from the robotic fingers.

"Relax, Jimmy," Superman said. He flew the young reporter up, up, and away from the robot. "You're safe now."

"Thanks, Superman," Jimmy stammered with relief. "I don't know why, but that big bucket of bolts seemed to be looking for me!"

"Hmm," Superman said thoughtfully. "I wonder why?"

"Beats me," said Jimmy with a shrug.

"I was just on my way to S.T.A.R. Labs," Jimmy continued. "I was going to take pictures of the Deep Space Probe for Clark Kent's story."

Superman set Jimmy back down on the sidewalk.

"First Lois Lane was attacked, and now you," Superman said.

"Is Miss Lane all right?" Jimmy asked.

"She's fine, Jimmy," Superman said. He stroked his chin. "Something strange is going on. I'll have to figure it out. But first, I have to stop that robot before somebody gets hurt!"

Before Jimmy could ask another question, Superman took off in a streak of red and blue.

WHOOOOSH!

The photographer raised his camera. He followed the Man of Steel through the viewfinder. He watched and took pictures as the super hero flew at the giant robot like a speeding missile.

Without pause, Superman tore through the side of the robot's metal head. Then he exploded out the opposite side.

KA-PANNNNG!

Only then did Superman stop to see the result of his attack. The giant metal monster came to a dead stop. Smoke and sparks spilled from the holes in its head. The menacing green glow of its eyes blinked off. Then, like a mighty tree that had been chopped down, it started to fall. Superman was there to catch it. Gently, he laid it down on the street so it wouldn't do more damage.

Jimmy was still taking pictures when he saw Superman's head suddenly snap up, listening. He knew the Man of Steel had heard something. In the next moment, Superman was gone.

THWOOOOMMMMMMM!!

He had flown away at super-speed!

"Wow!" Jimmy whispered.

CHAPTER 4

FLYING SAUCERS

"Great Caesar's ghost!" Perry White, editor of the *Daily Planet*, yelled from the doorway of his office.

Everyone in the newsroom of the great metropolitan newspaper froze. When their boss yelled like that, they knew someone was in big trouble.

"I just heard from S.T.A.R. Labs," Perry shouted to no one in particular. "The Deep Space Probe is about to land, and Clark Kent's not there to cover the story! Where is he?!"

Before anyone could answer, a loud noise filled the air. CRASH!! The windows all around the large room exploded in a shower of broken glass. Shards fell on desks and busy reporters. People shouted in surprise. Many dived under their desks for protection.

Through the broken windows came a swarm of small flying saucers. They were no bigger than dinner plates. They made angry buzzing noises as they flew.

BZZZZZZZZZZZZZZZ

One of the spinning saucers shot forward. It sliced through the computer monitor on a reporter's desk. ZING!

His face red with rage, Perry White stormed into the middle of the newsroom. "What do you think you're doing?" he shouted at the saucers. "Get out of here!"

The buzzing saucers reacted like living creatures to the sound of Perry's voice. They paused and then flew straight at him.

Perry stopped and stared. The flying saucers came toward him like a swarm of angry bees. BZZZT!

"What the —" he started to shout, too surprised to move.

Just before the razor-sharp saucers reached him, a hand reached out from under a desk. It grabbed Perry's arm and yanked him to the floor. The swarming saucers buzzed past his head.

The hand that had dragged Perry to safety belonged to Ron Troupe. He was one of the newspaper's newest reporters.

"Looked like you needed a hand, boss," Ron said with a smile.

"Thanks, Troupe," Perry said. "Remind me about this the next time you ask for a raise."

Perry lifted his head to peek at the saucers. They continued to swirl around the room. "What the heck are those things?" he asked. "And what do they want?"

Once again, the saucers seemed to hear the sound of Perry's voice. They made a sudden, sharp turn and came whizzing back toward him. Perry's eyes went wide with fear. He threw himself flat on the floor. But this time, the saucers dived down after him. He realized that they were tracking him!

Perry threw his arms over his head and closed his eyes. There was no escape this time. All he could do was wait for the razor-sharp flying saucers to find him.

Suddenly, the newsroom was filled with the harsh, loud screech of tearing and bending metal. Perry opened his eyes.

He looked up in time to see Superman, standing between him and the saucers. Several of them were already bent and smashed. They rested in a heap on the floor at Superman's feet.

WHAM! Another one was crashing harmlessly against the Man of Steel's invulnerable chest.

SMASH! Superman punched another one from the air. ZZRRRRRTT! The saucer clattered to the floor in a shower of sparks.

Superman shot his heat-vision at two saucers that were attacking Perry White. They instantly turned into melted hunks of metal.

BANG! SMASH! BOOM!

In a blur of super-speed punches, Superman smashed the remaining flying machines.

"Nice work, Superman," said Perry in relief. He rose to his feet, wiping his forehead with a handkerchief.

"Thank you," Superman said. "I wish I knew why my friends are being attacked. First Lois, then Jimmy, and now you."

"What about Clark Kent?" Perry asked with concern. "He's your friend too. And he never showed up at S.T.A.R. Laboratories. He could be in trouble!"

"Don't worry about Clark," Superman said with a smile. "I happen to know he's safe. And now, thanks to you, I think I know what's been going on!"

"That sounds like front-page news!" Perry said.

"It is," Superman said. "I'll make sure Clark Kent gets the whole story."

CHAPTER 5

FROM OUTER SPACE

The Deep Space Probe was blazing into the atmosphere high above Metropolis. It was traveling at many thousands of miles per hour. The thick layer of air surrounding Earth began to slow its speed.

Soon, the probe fell to a height of ten miles above the surface. A large parachute opened to slow it down even more. If all went according to plan, it would then float gently down to a soft, safe splash in Metropolis Harbor. Boats from S.T.A.R. Laboratories were waiting to pick it up.

At that same moment, S.T.A.R. Labs received a radio signal from the returning probe. Suddenly, the robot that Superman had defeated earlier came back to life!

Its large green eyes started to glow. The robot rose to its feet. It surprised the police and emergency crews who were trying to figure how to remove it from the street. Huge rocket engines in its feet roared to life. Like a missile, the robot blasted straight into the air.

RUMMMMMMMMMBLE!

Higher and higher it soared. Within seconds, it reached the Deep Space Probe, which was falling slowly to Earth beneath its large parachute. Like an outfielder catching a fly ball, the robot caught the probe in its giant hands. With its new prize, the robot began to return to Earth!

A tall figure stood in the shadows of a cavern beneath Metropolis. He waited patiently at the bottom of a large shaft that connected the cavern to the surface. He was waiting for something.

Sure enough, he heard the sound he was expecting. It was the clank of metal in the shaft.

"Come to me, my giant robot," the man whispered. He began to smile.

But the man's smile turned to surprise when the robot's head came tumbling out of the shaft! Wires and connecting rods dangled from beneath it. It had been torn from the robot's body.

The man jumped from the path of the tumbling head as it rolled across the cavern floor. It crashed against a rocky wall.

"What the devil?" the man growled.

"Not the devil," a voice echoed through the darkness of the shaft.

Superman came flying into the cavern. He landed in front of the man.

"Superman! What's the meaning of this?" the man asked. He was kneeling on the ground, brushing dirt from his dark suit. He stood up and stepped into the light.

It was Lex Luthor.

"I think you know, Luthor," Superman said. "After all, it was you who planned all those attacks on my friends to keep me busy. Meanwhile, your robot stole the Deep Space Probe."

Luthor smiled an evil smile. "I have no idea what you're talking about," he said.

"Having your men attack LexCorp first was clever," Superman said. "That way, I wouldn't suspect you. Not even after I checked the wreckage of your so-called Solar Generator with my X-ray vision. I wondered why you were showing reporters a fake machine made of useless parts."

"That proves nothing," said Luthor.

"Only you could have built those armored suits, and the flying saucers that attacked Perry White," said Superman. "And a robot with two computer-brains! You knew I would smash the one in its head to stop it. The second brain was in its chest. That one was programmed to steal the Space Probe!"

"What would I want with a ship full of space rocks?" asked Luthor with a sneer.

“Somehow you discovered that one of the meteors the probe was bringing back to Earth was made of kryptonite,” said Superman. “That’s the one thing in the universe that can kill me!”

“Hmm,” said Luthor. “I suppose the spaceship was lined with lead. That protected you from the kryptonite when you took the probe from the robot. Do you have any proof I did any of these things?”

“No. As usual, you were very clever,” said Superman. “One day you’ll make a mistake. When you do, I’ll be waiting.”

Luthor grinned. “In that case, I’ll be going now,” he said.

Superman smiled back. “One last thing, Luthor,” he said. “I’m afraid I smashed the elevator on my way down.”

"What?" said Luthor.

"Since you're such a genius, I'm sure you'll figure out how to fix it," said Superman. "Or you can just use the ladder. It's only a mile to the top!"

Superman waved and flew off. He disappeared into the dark shaft that led back to Metropolis.

Luthor growled. He could still hear the Man of Steel's laughter as he started the long climb to the top.